JO MAY

Let's be Frank

A horizontal view of an upright world

Copyright © 2023 by Jo May

All rights reserved. No part of this publication may be reproduced, stored or transmitted in any form or by any means, electronic, mechanical, photocopying, recording, scanning, or otherwise without written permission from the publisher. It is illegal to copy this book, post it to a website, or distribute it by any other means without permission.

This novel is entirely a work of fiction. The names, characters and incidents portrayed in it are the work of the author's imagination. Any resemblance to actual persons, living or dead, events or localities is entirely coincidental.

Jo May asserts the moral right to be identified as the author of this work.

First edition

This book was professionally typeset on Reedsy. Find out more at reedsy.com

For dogs everywhere.
Thank you for your companionship.

Also for Dad
who loaned me is laptop

Contents

Foreword	ii
Vital Statistics	1
Frankly Shankly	5
I'm a Porker!	8
Roots	14
Heaven Scent	18
Nutrition	22
The Boggart	27
Communication	34
The Working Environment	40
Cumbersome Yellow Things	44
Further Afield	48
Chatter	52
St. Bernard	55
Holiday Time	61
McTavish Wisdom	66
Bruce and Shanks	71
Year End	75
About the Author	79
Also by Jo May	81

Foreword

Dogs play a big part in today's world. I know, I am one.
 I can see first-hand just how much help humans need!
 During the recent pandemic every man and his dog acquired a dog.
 We helped share the burden of the world's collective madness.

I've put pen to paper because, throughout history, canines have been under-represented in the tower of literary babel.
 Here follow a few words that may begin to redress the balance.
 Enjoy.

Frank. 2022

Vital Statistics

My name is Frank and I am a dog.

I've called this little book 'Let's be Frank,' a title that offers a modest, yet worthy, touch of 'je ne sais quoi' (which is French for 'Could you pass the mustard?').

Right, who's Frank? Well, I'm approximately three quarters terrier and a quarter poodle. Does that make me a pooter or a troodle in the new lexicon of designer dogs? Don't know, but what I can tell you is I'm basically a sort of dark grey colour with a few lighter patches. Some reckon there's a bit of Patterdale about me. That's OK - it's a fine breed, originating in Cumbria. I'm not large or medium. But, neither am I small. Medium/small sums it up, I suppose – like Dad's intellect (I exaggerate). The poodle side isn't dominant and thankfully I look like a terrier - but the poodly bit means I don't lose any hair (unlike Dad). (By the way, just found out that Terripoo is the official breed name. Not having that!)

I'm fiercely independent, somewhat feisty at times, yet sensitive. I've just recovered from an injured front leg sustained while chasing (but failing to catch) our postwoman. If she hadn't leapt into next door's porch, I'd have had her sack. She's from Ontario, Canada which is a long way to come to get growled at. She tells Dad she feels welcome in England. Or did till we moved onto her beat and I tried to savage her.

I'm actually quite spry considering I'm thirteen years old, though bursts of speed are less frequent and shorter in duration these days. A 10-yard sprint every couple of days is about it. I jest. I'm better than that, and in the early mornings have been known to give the fox and deer a run for their money. (Not much money, I grant you … loose change rather than folding.)

I live with Mum and Dad in Littleborough. It's officially a village, rapidly becoming a metropolis, nestling in the foothills of the Pennines. When I say nestling, it actually looks like it was built on top of the hill and slithered into the valley. Surfed to a lower level, if you will, on a giant mud slide. It's now lying in an untidy heap among hills that looked down on Satanic mills till Fred Dibnah knocked them down. There's a canal, a (little) river and a main road in and out. Nice place.

Before we moved to our bungalow we lived on a succession of boats that got progressively rustier. Then, unbelievably, it went downhill as we moved into a knackered old camper van while looking for a house. We eventually found one and moved into bricks and mortar, albeit briefly, while they did it up. I almost said 'improved it,' but stopped myself just in time! Ultimately, Dad wasn't happy. Turns out it was a poor investment. In fact, he says it was the only house outside Beirut that went down in value in 2015. I prefer houses because I have an aversion to water. I said some unpleasant things about water when I was young and have feared a revenge attack ever since.

During my youth I spent years 2 through 7 trying to avoid falling off the aforementioned boats while travelling on a variety of murderous waterways. This was in the depths of France where it gets up over 40 degrees in the summer and minus 15 in winter. It's called a continental climate, I think. Well, if it is, it can stay over there. The interludes between roasting and perishing were OK but we all developed a strong meteorological constitution. Anyhow, that's all behind us now – hopefully.

I like it here and I've made friends. We have a real garden, rather than one that changed every day while traveling on the boat. I need familiarity; it was unsettling when we were on the move. I had to go out and find a new lavatory every day, and some of them were not as well maintained as they might have been.

Here in this little book, I'll tell you a bit about my mates and my uncertain relationship with humans. We call them 'Uprights' and, as we'll see, they can be a bit unpredictable, even cantankerous at times. I'll generally just ramble on about this and that, show you what it's like to be horizontal in an upright world. I get my material from four main sources. Firstly, general observation as I mooch around the area. Secondly, by closely observing Dad, who is reasonably representative of the Uprights, if rather towards the eccentric end of their spectrum. Thirdly, the canine Internet, colloquially known as The World Wide Wag, or Wag for short. And lastly my daily newspaper, which is perhaps the most intriguing source of information.

Yes, I go out and read my newspaper three times a day, four

sometimes. I troop round the park and playing fields with Mum or Dad (sometimes both if they haven't had a row) and find out what's been going on at ground level. From a distance my paper doesn't change much from day to day, but look closely, take trouble to read it, and you'll find each new edition is very different. I'm familiar with most regular contributors, friends who've had a pee here or a poo there, folks who's smells and signatures have become familiar. *'Ground zeer-eau',* as Sam (Basset) calls it. Sam is our resident humourist. 'I'm not really funny,' he tells us, 'it's more that everyone else isn't.' A talented chap, he's also putting the finishing touches to a musical about a chap who can't hold his drink called, *'The Wrath of Grapes'*.

We each leave messages for those who follow – it's an ever-evolving newsreel. A conveyor of piddles and pongs that defines our existence. It's a bit like that segment at the end of The Generation Game on TV - with whiffs instead of rubbish gifts. While we're at home Mum and Dad know what goes on in my world because they can keep an eye on me, but when I'm allowed to wander me and my mates share a world of enigmatic puzzles. Much like in the Upright's bailiwick, males are the biggest gossips (though they usually try and accuse the women of nattering the most). That's called 'transference' and typical of males who won't own up to anything. Males, in particular, constantly squirt piddly messages everywhere. It takes some concentration to figure it all out, I can tell you. It's an ever-changing web of clues and conundrums.

Frankly Shankly

Recently, it's been boiling hot and I've had a touch of hay fever – not good for a creature that makes a living with his snout. Dad tried to sneak two opiates into my food the other morning. I saw one packet – worming potion! As if I haven't got enough worms already – damn cheek. It turned my breakfast into a nasty grey sludge so I left it well alone. 'Ungrateful git,' he called me! Now I think back, perhaps he was trying to give me an antihistamine as well so I was a bit hasty sloping off in a huff. And I was hungry by mid-morning.

It's also been very bright, so much so I've had to wear my doggles. I did look pretty cool, if I say so myself. I was accused of being a poser by Betty (Dalmatian). I shuffled round her till she was facing the sun. As a consequence, she had to screw her face up in a squint. She didn't like this, I could tell. She is very prim and proper is Betty, very image conscious. Always has her spots nicely aligned.

'There,' I'd said, having waited till she could barely keep her eyes open in the bright light. I had the assured air of someone sporting the appropriate equipment for the conditions and went for the kill. 'Want to buy a pair? A hundred and forty to you.'

She flicked her elegant head and minced away with a wiggle of her back end, pretending that she wasn't developing a headache and her eyes weren't watering. She's a good mincer is Betty and can come across as a bit haughty. But under that elegant coat she's a real trooper.

Bruce (Lurcher) left a message in error the other day on the 'No Golf Practice' sign on the football field. He falsely accused Monica (Husky) of depositing a log outside number 14 on Central Avenue. Turns out it was a chocolate bar, probably jettisoned from a passing pram. Bruce later apologised, admitting that his actions had been misguided. He acknowledged that leaving an erroneous public message on a signpost had indeed been a cock-up. In fact, he was lucky. Monica's a big lass and could have made Bruce eat his own words. Thankfully, she's a fairly good-natured soul and only gave him a gentle nudge in the goolies. Bruce was last seen sloping off to lick his wounded privates in the privacy of a rhododendron bush.

Messages can be important. One friend, Shankly, is football mad. Shankly is his nickname, so called after the famous Liverpool Football Club manager back in the 1960s and 70s. He's actually called Arnold, though he hates that. He identifies as a Bichon Frise - when in fact he looks more like a mixture of an unraveling ball of wool and a ferret. I say *'identified as'* to be politically correct. You have to a bit careful these days. It's a funny one because some of the uprights have bits chopped off intentionally to change 'she' to 'he', or vice-versa. The majority of us hounds have had important parts removed - invariably without consultation. As a result, we find it difficult to comprehend that the Uprights undergo these procedures voluntarily. To be honest, after we've been 'tinkered with' we're not sure what we are. The atmosphere hereabouts is tense when one of us has to go to *Nipples and Knackers* for 'treatment.' We know all too well what's in store so the mood is sombre in the shire. We know that Fred may have an 'A' added on or Simone an 'E' removed. Brrrr .... doesn't bear thinking about. Me? Well, I was 'sorted out' many years ago before I was released from the dog pound in France. But I'm definitely a 'he,' albeit missing a couple of vitals.

Unfortunately for Shankly, his owners don't have the slightest interest in our national game. They prefer to watch programmes about properties they can't afford. As a consequence, our football-mad friend relies on the rest of us for updates, particularly during major tournaments (if we qualify). Quite a character is Shankly. His breed name is French and Bichon Frise translated means 'curly lap dog.' He hates this and would rather consider himself a burly central defender. He makes all the right noises but his physique lets him down a bit. I have to say that although I like to see our England lads do well, I find it a bit frustrating that eighty percent of the match is spent passing the ball sideways just inside our own half. It's not just us, it's everyone. 'Building from the back,' Shankly tells me indignantly. When I asked him why they can't build from the front he got a bit arsey and I was subjected to a foul-mouthed tirade in the scouse tongue. A meaningless rant designed to cover up the fact that he couldn't answer my question. I've come to the conclusion that if all the worthless rhetoric spoken about football was focused on world malnutrition instead we'd all be fat as pigs within a fortnight.

That's it for now. Toodle-loo (or 'to the loo' as we say).

I'm a Porker!

Been to the dogtor for an MOT. Bit unfortunate really - I'm officially fat! Ten percent too heavy, she says. Eleven kilos rather than ten. The Wag is a valuable source of lifestyle pointers. Fitness, we read, is in the mind. General well-being means being in control of your body and thoughts. Positivity, optimism and a forward-thinking attitude, that's what keeps us young. That, plus about 22 hours sleep a day (and as much food as we can get).

You'd have thought this rude intervention by my Health Care Professional a perfect opportunity to give me a dietary makeover. A little smoked salmon perhaps, the odd chicken fillet, a succulent steak. But oh no, what do they do? Give me smaller portions of the filth I've been getting since we came back to England. It's processed stuff, quite likely horse, that's had the life pummeled out of it by machines. There's a picture of what's supposed to be a happy-looking dog on the can. In truth it looks like the poor creature is at the point of death, having sat on a live railway line. The photo is immediately above the sell-by date, which is four years past my life expectancy so it's hardly likely to be fresh, is it? In fact, there's only one breakfast worse than mulched up horse, and that's Dad's. He often has fish. Fish for breakfast,

I ask you ... usually mackerel. He flavours it with all sorts of seasoning to hide the underlying taste. The only way it could possibly get any worse is if he ate sea-horse.

Let's be Frank - how am I supposed to function at optimum level when I'm fed dead horse? It's hardly surprising that when we're out and about I supplement my diet with morsels left by Uprights who can't be bothered to put them in a waste bin. And I'm not the only one - we all search for titbits. Sam calls it our 'horse d'oeuvre,' which I though was quite witty.

Oh, yes, I've just remembered. The Uprights have this fatuous turn of phrase they use frequently: 'I'm so hungry, I could eat a horse.' Don't think so, but you're welcome to have a plateful of mine! Actually, I was reading on The Wag last week that some local meat supplier was passing off horse as something else. Perhaps that's why horses gallop past our house at such speed - that's across the field with signs that say 'No Horse riding'! I've analysed this 'signs and what they mean' phenomena in a later chapter called 'The Working Environment.' Anyhow, back to health matters.

To make matters worse with my check-up, there's a pretty glaring spelling mistake on the appointment card. 'Annual check-up,' it said. What's the first thing that they do? Stick a finger up my rear end, that's what. Yes, spelling error here, people! Take an 'n' and a 'u' out of Annual – and you get a clue as to the real purpose of the visit. I'm only medium-small and that was one mighty substantial finger. Imagine, I said to Dad as we limped away down the road (well, at least one us us limped and it wasn't him), imagine sitting on a fat lamp post - that's what I've just endured. No sympathy came from that quarter; he just moaned about how much he was paying for my check-up. Miserable bugger, I haven't exactly cost them much over the years. Except the two eye operations which necessitated an overnight stay each time, then follow-up appointments, and one of those ridiculous conical collars that looks like a lamp shade, and make eating anything nigh impossible. I think those interventions may have dented his wallet, but I'm worth it. So I tell him.

He did get rather ratty one morning while I was in recovery mode. I was wearing my lamp shade and pottering along as I do, nose to the ground, sniffing out burgers, when I inadvertently hoovered up a dog turd into my collar. Caused a bit of a mess actually and we had to have a good bath when we got home. In fact, it went all over my proper dog collar too, the one with the metal tag which says 'If found please put on a ship to South America.' It just wouldn't come clean so he had to fork out for a new collar as well. That DID set him off grumbling, I can tell you. Still, I'm worth it, I told him again. (Not sure how long I'll be able to use that phrase without a kick in the rear!) Anyhow, I'm thirteen now so, all in all, apart from being porky, I'm fit as a butcher's dog. Apart from the slight hitch with the worms, and the hay fever.

Having recovered from my morning ordeal (with the help of a 3-hour nap) we went out for our lunchtime walk. Within minutes I'd picked up a whiff of discontent. Looks like they're thinking of build a new school on our playing fields. There were some pretty indignant messages from the canine quarter, I can tell you. Lucy (Collie) said she heard on the grapevine (she likes a tipple does

Lucy and spends rather too long by the grapevine) that they'll build on the football pitches then compulsorily purchase some nearby houses, which they'll flatten to make new playing fields. Wouldn't put it past them. She's funny is Lucy when she's had a drink. The Uprights are bad enough trying to cope with their two legs, but four? Well it can be a right old shambles.

Shankly was livid, I can tell you. Caused a right stench, leaving angry messages on every bush between the park and the woods. He does this when he gets riled, sort of lets fly like one of those intermittent garden sprinklers. Better not tell you exactly what he said, save to say that his language wouldn't have been accepted by The Kennel Club. But he has a point. It's not just us hounds who enjoy the open space, it's Uprights of all ages too. Some older folk stagger about, some jog, some chase dogs that won't come back. A few actually walk normally. On the other hand, I can see the need for a new school. Problem as far as I see it is too many people in too small an area. Dad has lived hereabouts, on and off, for over sixty years. He was complaining the other day that he really has to pick his times to take his failed woodwork projects to the council tip. 'Set off at the wrong time and you could die of starvation stuck in a jam,' he complained. Which sort of made sense. Like dying of thirst in a puddle. I hear that the local council has allocated a quarter of its annual slush-fund to fund the new school. A few million here and there, pah! Rogues the lot of them.

Bit reflective is Dad today. Lost his best friend on this day a couple of years ago. Dad's not the fittest specimen, so he was a bit unsettled when his mate succumbed. I met him, Alan, good man he was. Make the most of life, that's what I say. Seeing a big bloke like that crushed by illness was heartbreaking. Choked me up a bit, too, because Dad dedicated one of his books to his Al and his wife. Julie - she's a widow now, poor lass. Dad only got the book finished just in time. Being a bloke Al didn't react too much, but I think he was chuffed.

Actually, I can see him laughing - which is a great way to remember people. A couple of years ago Mum and Dad were trundling round in an ancient camper van while looking for a house to buy. To help things along, for when we stopped off somewhere, they bought a portable dog cage made out of metal tubes and canvas. The idea was to put me in it when visiting somebody so I wouldn't eat their furniture. Dad only ran over it with the van, didn't he! Damn good job I wasn't in it. I can see Al helping Dad try and repair it with a few screws and some sticky tape. The repair didn't work and the whole thing went in the bin. Much laughter. We'd bought the cage en route to Al and Ju's house - in fact, we'd only had it three hours before it went in the skip! Thirty quid down the drain. More muttering from Dad. The pet shop owner thought all his birthdays had come at once when we went in to buy a replacement. Dad was thinking of complaining that the cage hadn't been strong enough, but thankfully Mum talked him out of it. Could easily have made a fool of himself. Not for the first time.

The other thing of note recently is that they've finished doing up a house. Not to live in - to sell on and make another loss! Not seen too much of them recently, particularly Dad who has been coming home covered in dust for five months. I have been left to guard our house. Made a bit of a mess of the blinds, though. It's a bad habit. I've not got many adverse behavioural traits but this is one of them. Whenever anyone walks past I spring off an arm chair and leap at the window. I'm only doing my civic duty but if the blinds are drawn, too bad, they are just collateral damage. Mind you, they don't make 'em like they used to - about as feeble as my cage. The blinds are those vertical hanging ones. Ours are not in the best of nick, there's the odd slat missing. Look a bit like Dad's teeth to be honest. He's been busy these last months so he's taking it easy for a spell – doesn't half get under my feet at home though.

To try and keep fit (or less knackered) Dad does plenty of walking. We've had a very cold spell recently, snow and ice and all. He rather overdid it, I think, and has damaged his feet. So for the past week he's been struggling a bit on our sorties. Imagine a rotund blob limping on both legs, swaying from side to side and you'll get the picture. It appears that therapy for poorly feet is sitting down watching TV with a bowl of peanuts, particularly when there's snooker or rugby on. In fairness, he did pretty well up to the point the weather turned. I'll give him that, he does try. For a number of months he was on a regime he called his 8-day 50:50:2:1. Translated, it means that over an eight-day period he walked 50 miles, cycled 50 miles, drank 2 litres of red wine and ate a pound of peanuts. His doctor told him, 'Well, it started off OK ...'

I did 3 miles every morning with him, then at least another one during our lunchtime and evening walks, meaning I totaled over 30 miles in 8 days. Which isn't bad for an old gimmer.

Roots

It might be worth mentioning where I came from. To be honest, it was never certain I would turn out quite as well as I have. Modest, eh? Actually, those weren't my words - they were spoken by Madalene. She's known as Mad Lynn for short. McTavish the Scottie nicknamed her that. Ha! Save to say the two have **NOT** been best of friends since. There's only an 'A' missing from her given name, but one letter can make all the difference. Take the word clock, for example. See what I mean? That's what Mad Lynn called McTavish!

Anyhow, she is a very attractive Afghan Hound who is always well turned out in her posh coat and mane of luxurious hair. She's a good friend of mine, not because she thinks I'm well grounded. No, it's because I once lent her my doggles when she had conjunctivitis. A simple act of kindness for which she's been disproportionately grateful ever since. We've talked and messaged each other many times over the years and she knows where I came from and why I can be a bit unpredictable at times. I'm actually French, though I don't admit that to everyone. Especially now the United Kingdom has become a satellite nation off the coast of Europe. And, is it really a UNITED Kingdom? Not if you listen to McTavish. If it was up to him the Scots would still be marauding!

I was a dog of 'La Chasse,' which means The Hunt. When I was young, not even one year old, I got sent into the long grass with other dogs to flush out any prey that may be hiding in there. I really didn't enjoy it at all. The idea of chasing a rabbit out to face the guns of the land owners was sickening. So I just sat with the animals and kept them safe. One day I got caught chatting with a hare and that proved the end of my involvement with La Chasse. In fact, I was booted off the farm altogether as 'not fit for purpose.' I lived on the streets for a few months before ending up in the dog pound. I'd been there quite a while and was just about at the end of my tether when Mum and Dad turned up. An hour later I was on a boat in the middle of a lake. I didn't like that at all, and misbehaved all I could to get sent back to the pound. But they persevered, and I'm glad they did because I eventually got used to it and lived happily ever after! I wish!

I still get tetchy when I'm given a biscuit and someone gets too close. You see, when I was living rough in Dijon, Burgundy, food was hard to come by and I had to be very protective. Funny how things stick in the psyche after all this time. It perhaps explains the behaviour of some of my mates. Those who have 'less well rounded' personalities anyway. Like Bruce the Lurcher who is rather hasty with his remarks. He blurts out all sorts of ill-thought-out things. Some of us think he may even have a touch of Tourettes. Actually, he and I have things in common, in that he was bad at his job too. He was a poacher's dog and, like me, he sympathized with his prey so would bark whenever they got to the business end of a hunt. Each time he spoiled a 'kill' by barking he would be beaten into silence. Very nasty old farmer who owned him. Eventually he, too, was booted out and made his way to a rescue centre. We think that being silenced by force is why he chatters so much now. We share a dark cloud in our pasts and have unspoken empathy with each other.

Then there's Lucy the Collie, who likes a drink. Her owner used to be a pub landlady so our Lucy got her nose in rather too many drip trays. Even though her owner has now retired, Lucy still goes back and has a lunchtime tipple. More than a tipple sometimes. When we hear her singing 'Show me the way to go home' while lurching across the footy pitch, we know she's had one too many. She doesn't get nasty though, just giggly and funny. 'I don't drink any more,' she tell us regularly. 'I don't drink any less either.' Titter, titter.

Yes, things shape us. Mum and Dad have lived in four countries in recent years, and I joined them for the final three. They lived in Holland for a couple of years with their previous dog Bonny, my predecessor. She was a writer too and added her take to the books Dad wrote about their boating days. Actually, more than 'added to,' because without Bonny's shrewd, insightful passages they would have been turgid tomes indeed! (Don't let him see this for goodness sake!)

I joined them in France after Bonny had passed over. They have a photo of her and she looks a friendly character. I look forward to meeting her in the wonderland beyond the clouds. Not just yet though! I wonder if they'll keep a photo of me? We've had some lovely experiences. I love living in England but I think France was my favourite when we were travelling on the boat. Terrified as I was of the water, the food kept me going. Some lovely titbits could be found around the cafes. Some dropped, some begged for! My favourite was Cock o' Van, which doesn't sound very appetizing but had a wonderful flavour. I liked Cross Ants too – I'm partial to a bit of buttery pastry, particularly if they put a bit of jam on it.

Belgium was also a nice place. Problem is that their staple diet is chocolate and I'm not allowed that. Had to make do with french fries, or frites as they call them. They put mayo on them, which I didn't really like. The other thing is that Belgian Uprights are very orderly and tidy so they were less inclined to throw food on the floor.

Heaven Scent

Right, there's an intruder on the block, a mouse in the house so to speak. Actually, it's a fox. More than one, in fact. Foxes are not only bigger than mice, they are also more cunning. Can a mouse be described as cunning? I've heard tales of traps unsprung, empty of cheese. Does that qualify as cunning? Or just lucky? Is it better to be a lucky mouse than a cunning one? Maybe we've been underestimating mice all along. Conundrums. Well, I quickly drifted off topic there, didn't I?

How do I know we have a fox lurking around the fringes? Well, it's not pleasant, but I got too close to Alfred (King Charles) and he'd obviously had a roll. Phwoar, what a pong. He'll be in the doghouse when he gets home. Vulpes vulpes won't catch on as an aftershave that's for sure.

Despite being similar physically to foxes, neither me nor my mates can read their language. It's a complicated tongue, not unlike Cyrillic, and it's a bit frustrating because they are prolific message-leavers. Did you know that Cyrillic was an alphabet invented by Saint Cyril. Go on, check it out! Cyril lic, see? With that 'lic' at the end, perhaps Cryril was a dog? Anyway, most of foxy's messages are rather 'ripe' (to be polite) and a number of us have fallen foul of their scent. The problem is, fox messages are so pungent that they overpower everything else. Subtle notes are missed in the stench. For example, I almost failed to notice Julie's post announcing her being with child, ironically at the base of the 'No litter' sign. Then Doug ('the Pug') announced he was selling his collection of short-sleeve sweaters. I'm sure the disappointing response to his adverts was due to his message being asphyxiated by the ministrations of Mr Fox. He was trying to raise funds to send his sister Doris to Cheltenham. Never did find out why. Perhaps she had a horse running?

When we get to fox territory on our walks I try to creep up on them but Dad usually makes a racket to scare them off. He does this scuffing of feet thing and has a bout of pretend coughing. I don't think he wants me too close. Anyhow it works, by the time we get there all that's left are lingering scent trails and the odd stronger-smelling package. One time, to show my displeasure at him spoiling my fun, I had a roll, but the plan backfired. He was so furious he tied me up to the dustbin back home and gave me a cold water shower. I haven't tried since. Meany.

McTavish is a great message-leaver and amateur philosopher. When he moved here he was nicknamed 'The Preacher' but we've renamed him Messiah, with emphasis on the mess! We just about got away with that, but initially we'd named him MuckTavish. That didn't go down well at all and he threatened to bring a hostile army from the north. Anyhow, after that unsettling start he's fitting in well. He has a favourite bush near the cut-through; a well-chosen spot on a busy junction where he's a chance of being widely read. The bush is a peony, ironically enough, and we all look forward to McTavish's widdly wisdom. His messages often initiate heated debates. Sometimes we think he's just a troll, the like of which you'll find on the World Wide Wag. There's a forum in the Wag called Discuss Dog, a title that sums it up nicely. For example, he posted a notice on his bush the other day mocking meat-haters: 'I'm neither vegan nor vegetarian but I absolutely respect the right of the individual to be a pallid and spotty snowflake resembling a vitamin-deficient stick.'

You'd think that canines would definitely be meat-eaters, omnivores at least, but it's been surprising the number of hounds who have come out as veggy. A significant minority of nut-eating mutts avoid the butcher's cuts (that was a bit of a mouthful!). I've given the matter consideration and asked myself if I could go without meat. Basically no, except when Dad buys the budget tinned stuff. I know it's horse, but try and put it to the back of my mind while I'm eating. But I'm sure, by going veggy, I'd miss my meaty gravy and chicken titbits when the Uprights are having a roast. Plus the fact that it seems criminal to waste of a good set of teeth, evolved over millennia for the very purpose of tackling meat. Maybe that's a poor argument - you can after all cut a sprout with a steak knife. But it does seem criminal to waste a million years of evolution. Enough, it's making me hungry.

I posted a question on the Wag asking about foxes habits and what they do, apart from being prolific poopers. Hamilton (Rottweiler cross - so named because his owner, Gloria, likes Formula One) replied that they are quite useful because they eat vermin, including squirrel. Tell you what, though, they must be pretty quick because squirrel are nippy. I've had a go at catching squirrels and never really got anywhere near. Believe me, they are speedy little blighters. By the time I've got into top gear my quarry is usually about forty feet up a tree. I'm not a natural climber.

Hamilton is a bit of a joker actually, a bit of a wag you might say. He witnessed my failed attempts at squirrel hunting and left an old toy mouse for me with a note attached. 'Here,' he said, 'you might just be quick enough to catch this.' Very unkind. Foxes also like rabbit apparently. There's a wooded bank near the playing fields which you would have thought is ideal rabbit territory, but the cupboard is bare. I lay the blame at foxy's door.

Nutrition

Had a rather tetchy walk this morning. At least from halfway round when I got a telling off. I was sampling some horse poo – just too good to pass up it was, sitting there in a tempting pyramid right in the middle of the road. Not long deposited, it looked to be in its prime. The equine nuggets were almost impossible to walk past without having a root through and a nibble. Perhaps it wasn't as fresh as it looked. Thing is I ended up with the trots. Dad was furious, so I was banished to the garden for an hour till I'd realigned my digestive system. Though I enjoy the occasional taste of horse poo, it won't become part of my stable diet.

Saturday and Sunday mornings offer the most varied menu, particularly after the revellers have been out and about the previous evenings, depositing all kinds of tasty treats around the park and playing fields. Frankly, it's a joy for the discerning forager. Me going into the park is akin to Lucy discovering the Witch and the Lion in that magic land through her wardrobe. The aroma of burger and the aromatic scent of lamb madras all mix majestically with the pungent whiff of fox – what a sensory delight. It's always a bit of a battle at weekend – Dad tries to keep me moving; I want to linger and munch. It's like a game of push me/pull you, but life-or-death serious because food is involved. It's a pretty intense time because in between chomping and escaping Dad's boot, I have to leave messages for the gang. I always sleep well after my early weekend walks.

Dad and me walk in formation, me just off to the side and slightly behind. I've learned the skill off peeling off, like a Spitfire diving to begin an attack run, when I sense a tasty nugget in the bushes. It's about 50:50 whether he notices me gone or not. Sometimes he can be a hundred yards ahead before he realizes his wing man has disappeared. Then he starts shouting and whistling and I pretend not to hear. It's a game we play, though I seem to enjoy it rather more than he does.

I came across some frozen chips this morning. There was a hard frost and they were in a solid lump. I know Dad and his ilk buy frozen chips but I can't see the attraction of battling through a pile of frozen sticks. Not that I didn't try, of course. One of the dog's duties is to pass on information about today's menu. I take this particularly seriously because I'm usually the first up and feel I have a duty to inform my peers. Or is that peeers? Those who pee.

Being a rat catcher, I do enjoy a plate of rodent josh, but my diet is extensive and I'm prepared to try new things. In fact, I HAVE to supplement that stuff they feed me. If they served me chicken breast, do you think I'd scavenge and hunt the way I do? Yes, probably!

I tend to hoover and chomp my way round the three miles of our walk, constantly searching and grazing. Bert (right old mixture of breeds, but a playful lad) likens me to a caterpillar munching its way inexorably through a leaf. Bert's owner is a friend of Dad's, a nice chap who beckons his dog by shouting, 'Come on Bert.' Dad asked him why his dog has been named after a French cheese. It was a little witty that went straight over his mate's head. By the time Dad had explained it, the joke had died a death and been absorbed by the damp earth.

Actually, the guy has made a great recovery from a stroke and Dad became quite thoughtful by something he said. Though his friend appears completely recovered (apart from forgetting the odd word, perhaps … though we all do that) he knows in himself that there are things he can no longer do. I'm eavesdropping when I hear him tell Dad that there's fifteen percent of his former self that will never return. One of the most difficult things about trying to recover is that he is always mourning that portion of himself that he'll never get back. I find that very poignant and go and rub against his leg as a show of solidarity. It also tells me you never know what's going on inside, which is why I'm tolerant of my friends. Even Shankly, who can be a real pain in the arse at times.

Yes, a few of my friends have the unappetizing habit of eating poo. It's not for me but they seem to get a kick out of it. Live and let live and all that. There are few better soundtracks on a frosty morning than hearing Bert crunch his way through frozen dog turd. Ah, what a wonderful, varied world.

Dad enjoys a drop of the red stuff. Wine is a horrid colour, goodness knows what the attraction is, but he ploughs through it like there's no tomorrow. Never mind tomorrow, sometimes he can't remember the day before, so it all gets rather blurry. Anyhow, he had a bit of a disappointment the other night. There was a knock on the door. There stood our neighbour, nice lass, big smile, holding a bottle of wine. Oh, how lovely, thought Dad, wondering what he'd done to deserve such treatment.

'Could I borrow a corkscrew?' she said. 'I've just broken mine.'

To get over his disappointment, he had to have a reviver - a glass poured from a bulk-buy box of Welsh red he got from a warehouse in the backstreets of Rochdale. Quality gear, he assures us.

They've been on a health drive recently - more salads than flobbery, fatty stuff. I don't think either of them find it easy to change dietary track. To be honest, I think what they turn out looks pretty good. Mind you, compared to my mashed horse most things look good. I heard Dad talking to his mate out on the field the other day. He was saying that Mum is trying to inflict culinary manslaughter by serving up a series of dishes that look like rotting garden waste on piles of driftwood. He's only jesting, of course - it didn't look that good! Not sure they're not punishing themselves because they feel guilty about half starving me.

Dad had a go at cooking a couple of days ago. 'I'll prepare us a dietary dish for the ages,' he announced. Not only did it look like a bomb had exploded in the kitchen, he also managed to make an appetizing list of ingredients smell like an outside lavatory - with a blockage.

I didn't understand what they were on about to start with, but they seemed to favour a Low Carp diet. I wasn't even sure what a low carp was! So, I posted the question on The Wag. Turns out it's not Low Carp, but Low Carb. Someone explained patiently, 'That's Carb with a 'b'.' I'm still no wiser! Anyhow, the upshot is that they've had bucket-fulls of culinary 'misshapes' left over recently. They tried some on me a few times, but I preferred the horse. So you can see how bad it was. Fortunately, they have quite an efficient way of getting rid of waste material, including unwanted food - which just happens to be particularly abundant when Dad's been cooking! They put it all into a brown bin once a week, which is then emptied into a noisy, crap-eating monster that creeps slowly along the avenue. Crap-eating monster is an expression that could easily describe one or two porky Uprights I've encountered. No names!

The Boggart

One thing that I'd like to emphasise is that we dogs have special powers. In fact, we're quite an assortment of specialist packages who have evolved over the years into a pretty fearsome collective. Especially when compared to the Uprights, Dad in particular! If you think about, it we (canines) are rather amazing.

We come in a huge variety of shapes and sizes. Throughout the years, quite a number of us had our genes tinkered with to enable us to perform specific tasks. Such as rat-catching, or sniffing out drugs, or rescuing idiot Uprights who only find out they can't swim when they jump in a lake. What people don't realize is that these physiological manipulations only happened because <u>we</u> allowed them to. We knew that our gene pool, while remaining under the umbrella category of 'dog,' was developing to create a pretty fearsome collection of specialists. We could have stopped it at any time by simply sending in the heavy gang. But why, when we were developing into an assortment of super-breeds? I suspect that, ultimately, canines will endure long after the Uprights have blown themselves to bits.

We are a collective of experts all suffixed with 'dog.' The

Uprights are a collective of all sorts of random bits and bobs, many without a clear purpose. For example, we're readily definable by both appearance and behaviour. Humans pretty much look all the same and each individual is capable of a wide spectrum of astonishing behaviour, most of it questionable.

Our evolution is ongoing, but even today pound for pound, we are faster, hungrier, noisier, stronger and, yes, more intuitive. It's that last trait that is the most interesting. I ask the question to you Uprights: have you ever seen your canine companion stare into space, up into the corner of a room perhaps, and wondered what they are seeing? Granted, sometimes we are looking at spiders, the psychopathic dislike of which is one weakness we need to address in the breeding programme, but more often than not we are seeing something in another realm. The spirit of someone or something passed on. Sometimes a confused Upright who has come back to investigate what a mess they made of it first time round. We see some fairly despondent souls, I can tell you. That's why you'll see us looking up with mournful eyes.

During this dog/Upright evaluation I'm using Dad as a datum point. It's a bit unfortunate of course because it immediately puts them at a disadvantage, but we have to start somewhere. It's just that I get a good view of all Dad's inconsistencies. Not that he's the worst, mind you. No, there are 'even' worse examples than him.

I'm rambling again – let's get back to our special powers. That doesn't refer to horse power, although some of us are very strong, and fast. Instead, I want to concentrate on our powers of intuition and spirituality. In essence, we see things in an area of the spectrum unavailable to Uprights. To learn that they are lacking in intuition is not a surprise, but to find that we are far superior in some areas (or perhaps most) may surprise them. To illustrate this phenomenon, I'm going to tell you the tale of The Boggart.

So, what's a Boggart? Well, it's a creature that lives between myth and reality. A shape-shifting phantom that skulks in dark corners and takes on the shape of whatever is most feared by whoever gazes upon it. Not nice at all, really. Folklore to humans, all too real for us dogs. Dad and I walk in the park every day, early. He drags me out of the house at 5.00 AM so we see a world hidden to many - those that have the luxury of a lie in, for example! I envy them with some vehemence when it's chucking it down. During our walks, I read my newspaper. As discussed previously, it's an ever-changing newsreel of smells and sounds. My doggy friends leave a procession of pongs that tells us what's going on - including, from time to time, references to The Boggart. Dad isn't sensitive enough to pick up these messages. He just ambles along with a vacant expression on his face, humming songs from the 1970s.

Whenever there's mention of The Boggart, the doggy world takes a deep breath. Senses are heightened and piddles more pungent when The Boggart's afoot. In a state of ultra-sensitivity, I walk in the gloom of the predawn morning and see all sorts of shadows and shapes that lurk in the murk. Poor Dad, his mind was cast adrift many moons ago. He now dreams of what a great future lies behind him. Yes, we dogs pick up on The Boggart who lives in our park. The Boggart patrols by night, floating and swirling like a malevolent mist, weaving among the trees, rustling in the bushes. He stalks the deer, hounds the foxes and scares dogs.

But these days he only watches on - usually. A century ago, he was more sinister, wicked even. He frightened every living thing he encountered. He played on their fears, changed his form, personified their nightmares. The park was largely silent in those days and the only night-time visitors were unaware of The Boggart's existence, at least to begin with. These visitors only came once. After all, you don't want to come to a park to be confronted by your worst nightmare. It's almost as bad as seeing the Uprights during their first visit to the park in Springtime - when the sun shines hot for the first time and acres of puce flesh wobble like a meadow of shimmering blancmanges. Nearly as bad as that, but not quite.

Many years ago, a wealthy family owned Hare Hill House, the imposing property that is the focal point of our park. They also owned a monkey called Mephisto! A family pet, it is presumed. Sadly Mephisto died, aged two, when he supposedly fell out of a window. He is buried close to the house and must have been loved because his gravestone is still there today, tended lovingly by the park keepers. Mephisto is a creature of legend hereabouts. In fact, with a bit of imagination, Mephisto could be Littleborough's answer to The Loch Ness Monster. A tourism cash cow, if you will. Well ... with a lot of imagination, and not a cow.

For many months after Mephisto died, during the dark hours, The Boggart tormented the monkey's soul as it hovered between this world and the next. He teased and taunted and allowed him no peace. The Boggart persecuted poor, gentle Mephisto to the point where, one night during a torrential thunderstorm, the monkey's spirit fled. With a cry of anguish, Mephisto disappeared into the maelstrom, never to return. The Boggart had reclaimed his territory.

Many years later, close to his empty grave, a wooden carving was erected in Mephisto's memory. But all is not what it seems. Look into the monkey's eyes and you will see, deep within, the vengeful, smouldering eyes of The Boggart. During waking hours, the creature watches on, waiting for the night. When darkness falls he emerges into our world. Then beware, because a rustle of the leaves or a sigh in the tree tops may mean The Boggart is astir.

I sense him occasionally. I'm not really sure what he looks like. I see either a dark shadow or something in a form that scares me. He came once as a dog in severe distress, struggling to swim in a fast-flowing river. He knows I hate water but I've no idea how he knows. He somehow sensed my worst fear. During these visions he is never wholly distinct. Yet it is more than a mere impression. It's like an image you see in that time between light and dark, fading in and out of focus. Like looking through a steamy window. It's maddening that the picture is never completely clear, but it's certainly real enough and can chill you to the bone.

This is how he can unsettle me ... Last week, the day after my visit to the dogtor and the unfortunate episode with a digit up my back passage, he appeared in the shape of an enormous finger.

It looked like a ghostly airship floating among the tree tops high over the park. Now the finger episode at the docs didn't scare me as such, rather it left me indignant and embarrassed. The peculiar thing was that I somehow got the feeling that The Boggart was toying with me. In effect, it appears that he may have a sense of humour. Humour with a touch of malice. Time will tell.

What is inescapable is that every time I see him it gives me the shivers. His whimsical side is unconfirmed as yet. Surely he's not softening. For now at least, I'm erring on the side of malice. As Dad and me walk in the dark I can feel the confounded creature circling and watching. As night recedes, he returns silently to his lair, like a genie returning to a lamp. Get too close to the carved monkey in the half-light of early morning and we dogs can hear an ominous rumble from deep within. (Mind you, you'd probably grumble if dogs piddled on you regularly.)

Dad's oblivious to it all, of course. Can you believe he thought Boggart was something you hang in the downstairs lavatory! At moments like this I wish I was 'pretty vacant' too. Huh, see that? A sneaky reference to one of his dreadful musical fancies, by the Socks Pastils if I'm not mistaken.

He's so out of touch, he doesn't even know I'm writing this book. I'm getting my material from personal experience and in-depth research on the World Wide Wag. Amazing thing this Internet phenomenon that the Uprights have come up with. Just such a shame they use it for mindless babble. In the right hands it could be a life-changer.

I initially wrote this piece about The Boggart in response to an inquiry on my personal wagsite. I like to personalize things if I can, so I signed off ...

À Bientôt (which is French for 'See you soon.' In deference to my friend Sophie, a Picardy Spaniel, who made the initial inquiry after she thought she'd seen The Boggart for herself and needed confirmation. You'll probably meet Sophie in due course).

Communication

Canines communicate via an assortment of piddles and pongs. Yes, it's basic in method but also a subtle, if complicated, language that can be difficult to understand. All hounds have the in-built ability to communicate in 'mutterish,' the colloquial name for our language. The rudiments are passed from generation to generation and have transcended numerous evolutionary shifts. The Uprights on the other hand have developed this peculiar habit of talking to a thin rectangular box. Very strange it is, like me talking to a rock.

When we meet people face to face Dad's quite chatty and seems to enjoy himself - rather more than the opposition if the truth be known. But despite personal contact he insists on supplementing his chat quota by talking into his own box. I had to smile the other day; Dad was talking to an old chap who appeared less than captivated by the story he was telling. I could see the fellow's eyes glazing over, and at one point he turned sideways to stifle a yawn. As soon as he was able, at a point in the conversation where he didn't appear too rude, the man said, 'I'll let you get on then' and promptly set off down the road at some speed before Dad could start set off on another anecdote. The old guy's acceleration was commensurate with a Tesla in

'Mad' mode. 'I'll let you get on then,' is, of course, a polite way of saying, 'I've had quite enough of this prattling bozo.'

The Uprights have developed this complicated way of communicating with each other, apart from the one-way conversation with their thin boxes. They use a convoluted set of verbal expressions, idioms and noises. Sometimes arms get flapped for emphasis or there's some finger pointing. Dogs just have a few mannerisms. I think it's fair to say that our language is far more refined. We have a bark, which can indicate pleasure or annoyance, depending on whether we're smiling or 'baring,' or the wag of a tail or the cock of an ear. Then we have that doe-eyed expression when we're hungry. Dad is one of the few people able to resist that. 'Not yet,' he growls. 'On your bed.' I have to comply because a lack of disposable thumbs means I can't operate the tin opener to release my horse.

Dad's got a new doorbell, one that communicates with a noisy box in the kitchen. The sound it makes is a dog barking. It's quite realistic too - if a trifle mechanical - and of course, when I hear it, it sets me off. It usually erupts when he's settling down to watch his rugby and a parcel arrives for Mum. I haven't worked this out yet, but these parcels seem to originate from some river in South America. Perhaps it's a department store of some sort. There used to be one called River Island, perhaps they're related. The barking doorbell always seems to go off at an important stage of the match (or when he's nodded off). It's a regular ritual. The door chime goes off and he yells, 'Shut up you stupid dog!' By the time he gets to the door he's in a state of some anxiety and quite worn out. To be honest, it wouldn't matter what the doorbell sounded like, I'd still keep barking madly to wind him up.

Back outside again, I suppose the ideal doggy 'piddling post' is something inanimate or inorganic, but I can't help assisting in times of drought by peeing on the odd bush. But you have to choose wisely. This morning I was yelled at. 'Don't piddle on that - it's my sister-in-law's dead mother's ornamental Acer.' A tenuous relationship between tree and human if ever I heard one. As if I was supposed to know what an ornamental Acer is! It looked like any old mangy shrub to me, much like all the other mangy shrubs Dad's managed to de-cultivate. Is de-cultivate a word? It is now, and quite appropriate for the wilderness surrounding our house. I think you get the picture. There are also a few round dead patches on the lawn that he insists on blaming me for. I try telling him they're furry rings but he's not having it. I'm broad-shouldered, I can take it.

Our great advantage is that we can understand every word the human's say while they can't hear us. What it means is that we are pretty much in complete control. Depending on the mood or circumstance, we can choose to ignore them completely or be compliant. It's referred to as selective or targeted hearing. It causes them huge annoyance when we don't respond. I can see why. When they're red in the face shouting or whistling when we won't come back, I understand it may be a little frustrating. But if we come back just often enough, we'll be forgiven. It's a delicate balance but the key point is there may be occasions when we really need to ignore them. Like when we've found something revolting to eat under a bush. It's like placing weights either side of a fulcrum. Yes, I'll come back, no I won't, yes, no, no, yes ... The trick is to keep their frustration balanced in the middle.

COMMUNICATION

Communication between dog and Upright should be a simple affair. A basic set of commands and responses is all that's needed. Dad tells the story of his friend in France who owned an English Bull Terrier called Dozer – short for bulldozer. The dog had a tendency to do his own thing, much to Bob's frustration. The main problem was that Bob used 20 words where one would do. Rather than saying 'Sit' he'd say, 'Will you go and sit under that tree out of the way so I can read my book in peace?' There are a number of fairly obvious flaws in this command – lack of brevity being the glaring one. Mum tried to help and bought a packet of little treats. She would command, 'Sit'. The dog, with a little pushing and shoving, sat. Mum rewarded him with a treat.

'Come – Sit' – Perfect! Treat.

'Here Bob, you have a go.'

'Here Dozer, come and sit down.' Wag, nothing.

The problem was that Bob lived alone with Dozer and they needed to chat. One-word chats wouldn't cut it during long, quiet evenings. They both needed company. The training came to an end when Bob found a mouth-shaped chunk bitten out of the bottom of his paperback, rendering it unreadable. He threw the remaining treats at Dozer. 'Well, you bloody dog,' he said, and the training came to an abrupt end.

We canines have a bank of therapists or specialized service representatives on hand should they be needed. They cover anything from transport to psychiatric malfunctions. There are some diligent and creative characters around the neighbourhood. A recent innovation has been introduced by Hamilton, the Rottweiler cross. He realized that some of us need transport to various appointments, occasionally even to Nipples and Knackers - when the clients need all the help and compassion going. Some of us, perhaps the physically challenged, just need help to get from A to B, or to A & E.

Hamilton had a Eureka! moment and set up his transport business called Bark and Ride. Very popular it's proving, too. So now he pulls the needy around in a natty little 2-wheel trailer. Hamilton's creativity demonstrates we canines' versatility. He, of course, is the perfect specimen for dragging around heavy loads, so employs his attributes to common purpose.

Alternatively we have helpers who are more cerebral. One such is Alice, an English Pointer. She's not been here long but made an immediate impression with her abilities as a Medium. McTavish called her Alice Aforethought, which was quite clever. One or two of us took a while to get our heads round this. Doug the Pug asked, 'What the heck is so special about being medium? Surely that's just a quirk of birth. Nothing amazing about that.'

'Not medium as in size,' said Sophie (Picardy Spaniel), 'Medium as in Psychic.' Doug looked nonplussed. Shankly wandered up at this point and heard something that sounded like 'kick' so presumed the conversation was about football. But he, too, was told no - psychic, as in medium. 'Ah yes,' he said, 'we have psychics in Scouseland. They are often employed as marriage guidance councilors. They are very popular with brides to be who seek guidance as to whether their future husbands are likely to be rewarded with a full raft of social benefits. The concept has spread now to places such as Peterborough and Rochdale.'

'That's all well and good,' said McTavish, 'but most of our lot round here can't remember the immediate past, never mind seeing into the future.'

'That's exactly why you engage Alice,' said Sophie with typical Gallic common sense.

Just at that moment Dylan the Dachshund walked by. He always closely shadows his Upright, who enjoys a drag on the weed. The pair of them, spaced-out owner and wobbly-gaited dachshund, are usually immersed in a sweet-smelling cloud. Dylan insists he only gets himself stoned for medicinal purposes, claiming he has arthritis in his hips.

'Now there's a hound that doesn't give a damn about present or past. In fact, most of the time he won't be aware he even has hips,' said Sophie.

'Might be the way to go,' muttered McTavish. 'Just obliterate everything. Clear your mind of negative thoughts.'

'Or any thoughts at all. Like Frank,' said Doug.

The Working Environment

The Uprights seem to have a collection of jobs that don't mean very much. For example, they have somebody paint lines down the sides of roads in various colours and configurations. But why? It doesn't change their behaviour. Everybody just seems to abandon their vehicles exactly where they want, even half on and half off the pavement straddling the lines. It doesn't matter what colour or shape the markings are, people just ignore them.

They have this peculiar little word spelled, 'N O', pronounced 'know.' I can't really work it out, but it seems to give them permission to do exactly as they want. For example, on the field where we tramp around incessantly, the little word can be seen on signs preceding the words, 'Motorbikes', 'Golf' and 'Horses.' This seems to be a green light for anyone riding either a motorbike or horse to charge around the footy pitches at great speed. The chap practicing his golf recently wasn't proficient enough to be categorized as a golfer so didn't count towards the statistics. However, if he improves a bit, he'll become just another Upright ignoring a 'no' sign.

Similarly, the same little word goes before 'parking,' 'waiting,' 'littering' or 'entry.' Often these signs have a red line round them or a diagonal red slash. These red splashes of colour appear to emphasize that Uprights have a green light to indulge in that particular activity. The point is, why do they need the word that sounds like 'know' at all? All it seems to do is give them permission to do something. Unless of course the little word makes the accompanying action obligatory. You MUST litter here, for example. It certainly looks that way after a weekend of good weather when the countryside is full of all crisp packets and half-eaten burgers. Perhaps they could suffix the signs with 'Fine.' As in 'Parking Fine,' or it's fine to park here. Can't see why that wouldn't work.

Then there are those round signs with a number in the middle - 30, 40, 50, for example. It seems that these are minimum speed limits, designed to keep the Uprights on the move and the hospitals operating at maximum capacity. The lines, the 'NOs' and the number signs are all pointless as far as I can see. I'm sure the Uprights who create and install them all are grateful to get a wage. That way they can buy vehicles, and the fuel that makes them run, so they too can ignore the signs. I'm slightly perplexed, but have to admit the arrangement has a pleasant symmetry to it.

Just occasionally I see a Parking Warden. Huh, I thought at first it was Barking Warden, which is uncomfortably close to Dog Warden, someone we canines all try to avoid. I was wary about making too much noise at first, but it turns out the warden is some kind of enforcement officer connected with road markings and 'no' signs. Dad had a noisy encounter with a woman who'd fallen victim to a Parking Warden and had been fined fifty pounds. That's over three and a half stone! I thought that was a bit heavy for a minor indiscretion. Turns out it was a free parking area, at least for the first two hours. Thing is, you have to display a ticket to tell the warden what time you arrived. Well, she had! Her crime was that she'd put it on her dashboard upside down so the warden couldn't see it. I'm not surprised the woman was irate. 'Ill have your job for this,' she yelled at the warden. 'I wouldn't bother,' he'd replied. 'The pay's not great.' Which made her even more ratty. The Uprights do make things complicated.

My job is to piddle and leave messages in my role as a roving reporter. I'm just getting a business card together so am trying to find the appropriate word to accompany the word piddler. Inveterate, inconsiderate, prolific? As far as piddlers go, I'm one of the best. Prolific, I think. Yes, that's nicely alliterative. A simple card with a bone number and: Frank - Prolific Piddler (pity I'm not called Prank).

A couple of weeks ago I got myself in bother when I piddled on the goal post during a lads' football match. Problem was, it wasn't an eight-foot metal thing, it was one of the lad's coats. Dad was furious and embarrassed in equal parts. He took the soiled goal post home, telling the young owner he could collect it the following day after it had had a trip through the washing machine. To be fair, it was a bit of a lapse on my part. Problem is, anything poking out above grass level is prime territory for a piddle. Fair game, you might say.

What was particularly unfortunate was that Shankly was looking on. Just my luck. He was on a scouting mission, I think - on the look-out for young talent to have a trial with the Rose and Crown Under XIs. Anyhow, he witnessed my indiscretion and nearly wet himself laughing. Needless to say, he rushed off leaving squirty messages in his wake all over the neighbourhood. I had a couple of days of ribbing, dogged by childish sniggers and side-of-the-mouth mutterings.

Cumbersome Yellow Things

Last summer Mum dragged us to the park to listen to some music. Me and Dad were right in the middle of The Guns of Navarone, so he was a bit surly for a while. But the sun was out, the clouds were fluffy and the Brass Band were playing. A Brass Band is a largely northern thing where a collection of uniformed people blow through an assortment of cumbersome yellow things and make a racket. I jest - they're very good, and some of the players are young, barely out of short pants. In fact, some don't look big enough to lift their instruments, never mind get any noise out of them.

It was a snapshot of our village, both canine and Upright. There was an elderly couple sitting on deck chairs with blankets over their knees, despite the hot sun. They were each wearing a white floppy hat (probably a job lot from the pound shop) and chewing on limp sandwiches (from the three-for-a-pound shop), perhaps recalling the days when they courted in the same park many years ago - when a sandwich was made of door stops and beef dripping rather than cardboard and soggy salad. Mums and Dads lounged on rugs while the kids charged around the playground or played an impromptu football match with few apparent rules and no boundaries. And jumpers for goal posts. I looked at Dad, who said sternly, 'Don't give me the eyes. I don't care if you are a qualified referee, you're not going anywhere near those goal posts.'

I'm happy to relax and watch the world go by and I saw some of my mates out and about. One friend went past who goes by the unlikely name of Bolt, so called because he's got a screw loose. Not really, he's just young and full of life, not at all like me and Dad - we are elderly and full of aches and pains. Bolt is only a few months old but already huge. Best to keep on friendly terms with dogs that might end up the size of a horse.

Aahhhh, that's all a nice warm memory. Now we're up to date in the chill of winter. Speaking of things equine, Dad got on his low horse about something this morning (he can't get on a high horse these days.) Of course, I was involved, but did I really deserve the tempestuous ticking off I received? Allow me to explain. It was snowing a little and there was a healthy dusting on the ground. Dad got into biologist mode and lined up to photograph a fox's paw print. I wondered what he was up to and walked by for a closer look – and trod right on his subject matter. Good job there wasn't anyone about with a sensitive disposition because his language was less than gentlemanly, I can tell you. His mini-tirade ended with git, but there was worse before that! At least one little word rhymed with cough.

It's not like there aren't hundreds of foxy foot prints all over the field. And let's be honest, he normally takes a succession of out-of-focus mishaps which all end up in the bin. Perhaps he reckoned he'd got a nailed-on certainty with this one until I interfered. I've actually seen the final image and it does look like a blurred dog print which has trodden on an indistinct fox print, so he'll have to go back and try again anyway.

They have these things they call 'schools.' Their purpose, it appears, is to entertain the mini-Uprights. In fact, they've been building a new junior one (school not Upright). Not sure I quite understand, but it appears they are building it to replace one that is twenty yards away to the east. Then they are knocking the old one down and building another new one on a nearby football pitch. As Lucy pointed out the other day, 'There seems to be a wrinkle in their long-term planning strategy.'

'Unless,' said Bert, 'it's a rolling plan to keep planners, architects and construction companies in perpetual work. Perhaps they'll build a new library next to the existing one, then knock down the original?'

This is the same school Shankly was ranting about recently. Schools, apparently, are where they teach the youngsters to read and write so they can integrate and communicate with the world beyond. They are taught to be polite and respectful and be of tidy appearance. Doesn't seem to work too well, though, because whenever Dad comes across them, either singularly or in a group, and he greets them with a cheery 'good morning,' they invariably walk straight past without uttering a sound. Perhaps it's just him. Maybe he went to the wrong school.

One things we dogs do is live by instinct. We're all individual and sometimes unpredictable. Most of the Uprights seem to follow one another's lead, like sheep, only less attractive. If one behaves in a certain way, another one follows suit, then they all do. If one dresses in a style, they all seem to copy it. Mind you, I think my Mum must be quite a trend-setter. She wears these black stockings, or are they leggings, which I think must resonate with the youth of our town because I see some youngsters playing football wearing the same black stockings. Young lads this, not girls. 'Never happened in my day,' mutters Dad. But it does seem as if all individuality is being oozed out of them. Most have similar haircuts and clothing. They seem to follow trends set on TV where people with impossibly white teeth are paid ludicrous amounts of money to do all manner of embarrassing, mindless things. Like Crufts, for example. Mind you, Mum came home recently with pink hair and since then I've seen one or two others of a similar age also with pink hair. I think Mum is a trend-setter.

I don't even like wearing a coat when it gets chilly. I'd much rather go 'au naturelle.' They bought me one once, bit of an all-rounder with a furry hood called a Barka. First day out I rolled in a fox dollop and that was the end of that. Thankfully.

Further Afield

I was fortunate enough to be there on Dad's first outing with his new poles. I was rather sceptical because last time I was out with someone with a random piece of metal, Mum was waggling a coat hanger about trying to find water. The metal is supposedly attracted to underground water. Not sure about that, but she certainly attracted plenty of attention!

As it turns out I wouldn't have missed Dad's pole debut for all the tea in Yorkshire! It's usually just me and him, but today he'd added a complication that appeared beyond him. 'Walking Tech,' he termed it – 'trekking poles.' Gold ones they are, with lumps of rubber on one end (and an idiot at the other … shh!).

We've come in the car to a point a thousand feet up in the Pennines. From here, he tells me, 'We'll traverse the moors in a three-mile loop and be home for breakfast before the world wakes up.' Optimism of the first order this. It took him a quarter of an hour to cross the road to get to the launch pad. He puts me on the lead to cross said road as any conscientious companion would. But while trying to remove it, he somehow gets it tangled up with his poles and his ruck sack straps. To be honest, I'm not even sure the lead was necessary. Or the ruck sack. Or the poles. It's 5.45 AM and we haven't seen a single car in the five minutes we've been here. There's a lot of muttering before he finally disentangles himself. Anyhow, we are safe now, through a swing gate. 'Sheepside' is where we are, within a thousand-acre enclosure delineated by barbed wire and posts. A land where optimistic sheep roam free on rock-strewn tufty grass landscape. An alien land and wholly unsuited to a bloke with untested aluminium appendages.

We're at the bottom of a nasty little slope, a tricky climb up to our official starting point. It's a rocky track with which I cope admirably. I can hear him huffing and puffing somewhere behind. It's obvious that all is not going to plan because the odd swear word drifts up to me in the crisp morning air. When I turn round to investigate he's gone over sideways and is half-sitting, half-lying in a patch of track-side heather. He looks a bit like a green earwig that's been flipped over, waggling its legs about, trying to get the right way up.

This first 'pitch' should take us about ten minutes because frankly it's not that far, a couple of football pitches I would think, shaped in an arc round a hillock. Admittedly, it is steep. When he finally gets himself back on his feet he's blowing hard and we're still so close to the car that he could have thrown his poles at it. What he's done inadvertently by wearing his lime green cycling jacket is make sure that anyone within miles will pick him out against the shades-of-grey terrain.

I can hear him stumbling and grumbling behind me but finally he arrives at a flat bit. Cursing his new poles, he mumbles, 'Bloody things have a life of their own.' Then he realizes he still had the rubber protective bits on the bottom, which was why he wasn't getting the grip he expected. We've probably come about 200 metres, albeit it steeply uphill, but poor old Dad has to break out his rations to re-fuel. While he's having a drink a lady steams up. She's at least twenty years older than Dad, but her gait suggests someone thirty years younger. With a cheery 'lovely morning,' she bounces off down the track. 'Smart arse,' he mutters.

I wait patiently for him at the crest of the hill, then wait again till he is ready to continue. I do wonder whether he will turn round and head back down immediately, but he has a steely look in his eye so we set off again. He seems a bit more comfortable on the flat and settles into a stick-clacking, shuffling rhythm. He still looks rather self-conscious. Good job there's nobody about. Until there is. He's geared up for a Himalayan trek when we're passed by a young couple dressed not so much for a hike as a visit to a cafe bar, wearing trainers and trendy, lightweight threads. And they have a pair of athletic Labradors with them, dashing hither and thither. All four of them look ridiculously healthy and totally unconcerned that they are tackling a very demanding landscape unsuitably equipped. Healthy compared to Dad anyway! As they pass, Dad bends down and pretends to attend to a shoe lace. I don't think he wants them to see his face, unwilling to risk future recognition.

After half a mile on the level we turn left up the hill, on to an old Roman Road. Because his legs are a bit knackered (circulation), hills are Dad's enemy. I admire him, actually, for having a go and today he has his new poles to help. Do they? Well, a bit I think. It's pretty steep and this pitch is roughly a quarter of a mile. He's staggering up the cobbles looking like one of those things that landed from Mars in 'The War of the Worlds.' Vaguely menacing as he's hunched forward, madly driving his sticks into the turf and lurching from side to side. Yes, he's like H.G. Wells' invaders, just less coordinated ... and less threatening ... and noisier ... and slower. In fact, not much like an invader at all.

I'm coping pretty well; you have to remember I'm about ninety in Upright years. Actually, I'm a bit naughty because I ham it up a bit. I pretend to be more fleet of foot than I actually feel and skip about like a newborn lamb. Finally he can take it no longer. 'You can stop that as well.' he yells. 'You're supposed to be old! For Pete's sake, act your age.'

Up here on the moors it's just us, which is nice.

At least it would be if he was a bit quicker.

Chatter

A few days ago McTavish left a cryptic message on a goal post: *'Regarding further education – if we don't know what we don't know, how do we know what to learn?'* It had a few of us scratching various parts of our anatomy trying to figure out what he was on about. Sam reckoned he'd been on the malt, aggravating an already troubled mind. Perhaps the latest dram had finally broken the camel's back.

McTavish tried to explain (on the opposite goal post because the left hand one was now getting rather over-piddled with replies), saying that he was thinking of taking an Open University course and was doing some research on The Wag. Turns out he was trying to find out how much we didn't know, a subject about which there wasn't much to be found. My reasoning is that neither dogs nor Uprights can research what we don't know about if we don't know what we don't know. It's not surprising that there's not much information to be had. I suppose this was the gist of McTavish's confusion and, to be frank, the conundrum was rather spoiling my morning walk. As far as I can see, every one of us doesn't know more things than we know. So I said so in a brief message. 'I don't know what you're on about.' Hoping that would settle the matter. I hoped my message would trickle down the goal post into the grass and slowly return to mother earth – from where it should never have been dug up in the first place.

McTavish, poor lad, wasn't getting much help. As far as I could tell nobody came up with anything helpful at all. In fact, quite the opposite – he got a number of messages telling him to forget the idea of further education altogether. Alfred, the King Charles (known for his pithy asides) said, 'Never mind further education, he hasn't mastered nearer education yet.' McTavish got so irate that nobody was taking him seriously that we feared he'd lost the plot temporarily when he posted, *'You lot are nothing if not negative.'* That meaningless assortment of random words caused further communal scratching.

We haven't seen him for a day or two, so he's probably gone off in a huff. He's either immersed himself in The Wag or gone to visit his brother in Rochdale. I hope it's the former because I can't see Rochdale improving his mood. Truth be told, the episode of McTavish's education left us all feeling rather fraught. Step up Sam, resident humourist and mood-lightener general. He told us about Keith the Airedale. The breed, Sam informs us, is a large terrier. Now I know that small terriers, like me for example, are stubborn and independent-minded buggers, so Dad and I have this eternal battle of wills. Dad explained our skirmishes to his friend recently, after he'd just given me a fearsome shouting at. He was yelling so loudly his mate feared for my safety.

To reassure his friend, Dad quickly explained, 'We have plenty of altercations, the usual reason being that the dog ignores my calls to come back. It's maddening and every now and then I have to give him a proper bollocking to let him know who's boss.

Owning a terrier,' he continues, 'means having constant battles, most of which I have to win. The best you can hope for when we get to the final reckoning is to win enough battles for the overall war to end in a score draw.' I don't see it quite like that, of course. Dad thinks that I'm not up to speed with his tactics, but I am. I 'allow' myself one ticking off a month so the rest of the time I can graze around the neighbourhood searching out treats in relative peace. Ultimately, I know he wouldn't do me any harm. Our war is basically a polite one where we both win enough to be happy.

I'm off course again. Back to Sam's anecdote. Keith is owned by Mrs Driscol, a lovely lady who is rather timid, and a widower to boot. Sam said, 'By the time Mrs Driscol trained Keith to come back he was too old to go anywhere!'

That quip cheered us up. You never know when he's telling the truth or making things up, but he told us another tale the other day. He'd overheard two Uprights talking recently and one said, 'I just bought a greyhound.'

'Really? What you going to do it with it?'

'Race it, of course.'

'My money's on the dog.'

Things gradually returned to parity and McTavish's educational problem joined the mountain of other unsolved conundrums.

St. Bernard

We went out for a jolly ride in their new car. New to them anyway. A monster of a thing, basically a van with windows. I was crammed in the back with all sorts of paraphernalia, including his bike and a picnic hamper, and we set off for a random place in the wilds of Lancashire. The car was a much smoother ride than the knackered old thing they used to have and I was sick in the back. I managed to keep it off the new upholstery by vomiting in a basket. Had I realized it contained our lunch I would have had a choice to make, but I didn't ... so I didn't. Anyhow, I got sent to the dog house by Dad. Mum was a bit more forgiving because Dad had made the sandwiches and there was every chance they'd have been awful anyway.

After that first disaster, future trips improved considerably. Another place we went was a relative's house in the middle of nowhere in Cumbria. Some good ratting to be had there. Or would be if I was a bit more fleet of foot. It doesn't appear there are many arthritic rats in the North West, the type that give me a sporting chance - Latin name, Rattus Ponderous. The ones up here are speedy, Rattus Rapidissimus - which would be a mouthful if I could catch one! Rat-catching is actually in my genes, quite different from the hunting that Bruce and I did. Yes, I was born to it rather than having it forced upon me. Squirrels are another annoying breed, another branch of evolution quite safe from my ever diminishing powers.

There are some good walks to be had up there, lots of hills, plenty of sheep and some eccentric locals. As Dad says, he can walk for three hours and not see another soul. Mind you, that's only about two hundred yards. There are rabbits too, things we don't see round home - Vulpes vulpes has seen to that. There are fell ponies that wander from hill to hill. There's one group that travel together which is rather nice; you can see them way out in the distance. There's a single white one and the rest are either black and white or fully black. They stand out as little dots against the dusty green of the distant hills. Sometimes the white one travels in a twosome with a single black one, but for some inexplicable reason Mum calls the white one Billy No Mates, despite the fact that it clearly has a companion. Perhaps she thinks the black one is is not strictly a friend of the white one. Maybe it accompanies the other horse in a professional capacity, as a therapist or personal trainer, perhaps, or groom.

They are a hardy breed and have to cope with some pretty ferocious weather up on the hills: wind, driving rain, ice and snow. There are little copses of trees here and there which is where they must find a bit of shelter during the worst of it. Close up, the horses look a bit disheveled with all that excess hair round their feet and heads, but excess hair is a necessity up there where it can get mighty wild. For obvious reasons Dad has to wear a hat! Sometimes you can see the horses silhouetted against the skyline and I imagine them as a line of camels bearing their burdens, nose to tail, in the desert. In my dream they bring various gifts to the Son of Dog in his straw-lined kennel.

Dad writes the odd book too, you know. He's just come back from town where he had an encounter that put him in a bit of a mood. He asked the local bookshop what happens when he sells all the copies of his book. 'I'll order another one,' came the reply.

We dogs think that one area the Uprights have got it rather wrong is Religion. Taken as a whole, it's too segregated, complicated and combative. The reason I'm qualified to speak like this is that I can directly compare theirs to ours. For canines it couldn't be simpler - we have one deity who (usually) comes up with sensible ideas. There's one point of contact, one philosophy, one single point of focus - Dog Almighty. That's it. No argument.

The Uprights have five big religions all squabbling to be the biggest and best. Throughout the years, some of these squabbles have been vicious affairs. It appears that the only person guaranteed safety is the leader - everyone else is liable to be sacrificed on the altar of religion. 'Go on, away with you minions, fight for our common good. You will be remembered, revered and rewarded even though you end up in a hole in the ground many miles from home. Remember, we're all in this together.' Best to be a leader I reckon. It's further complicated because within those five mainstream religions there are numerous off-shoots.

We've discussed this in the shire; it's been piddled about extensively. I'm sure there was every reason for the arguments to become heated but fortunately, because we are so settled in our faith, we've basically come to the conclusion that the Uprights can squabble all they like and nothing we say will make any difference.

One thing we've realized is that anyone can start a religious splinter group. The group leader needs no specific qualifications, either theological or professional, save the ability to persuade people that their particular dominion in paradise is the most idyllic. By some strange coincidence, it becomes more idyllic the more money a new disciple throws at it. Yes, Uprights can buy eternal bliss. How good is that? In fact, if new disciples hand over all their money, they are given special privileges, such as being allowed to dig vegetables or have sex with their spiritual leader in a potting shed. Depending on how punitive the new group is, they may be called a cult or a creed. Cults can be a dangerous thing to get involved with, often with manipulative leaders smoking dodgy leaves. Other religious orders may be more benevolent. As far as I can ascertain, these less aggressive groups have a funding model based on the trading of home-made cakes and craft products of uncertain provenance. They flog their wares to the faithful in draughty halls in order that the vicar can upgrade his motor car every two years.

Let's take two main religions to try and explain the difficulties. The Christian faith is based on a book compiled by scribes. This book relates the exploits of a group of people, chosen apparently at random, who roamed the earth a couple of thousand years ago performing unlikely tasks and preaching to the convertible. The Uprights, in their current incarnation, have been around for about 200,000 years so it seems peculiar that it took 198,000

Christmas Days for someone to arrive deemed worthy of writing about. Mind you, when they did finally make an appearance, it's pretty impressive that one man and his son gathered so many followers in the blink of an evolutional eye. According to the scribes, the son did all sorts of amazing things. People like a good story – I think that's why their book sold so well.

The Muslim faith is nearly as big, but growing, whereas the Christian faith is just about holding its own. It appears this is because Muslim converts are promised a selection of carnal treats in the promised land beyond the clouds, including seven virgins – believe it or not! The afterlife must be very different to nearby Rochdale – you won't find that many virgins there. Seems a bit random to me because these virgins could be male or female and it's pot luck what the sacrificial lambs end up with. Anyhow, that little quirk notwithstanding, they presumably have just as many extraordinary stories to relate, plus an interesting variety of nutty offshoot sects. They are quite open about funding, exemplified by the fact that the main leader is called a Profit. Their guidebook relates equally incredible feats of godly exploits, but it also seems to include a few verses that people take literally and can cause international chaos. Actually, I think my favourite religion is Cat Holic. They have this liberal attitude where you can do whatever you want, then absolve yourself by saying a few Ale Mary's.

You see, none of these religions is straightforward. They are open to interpretation and thus abuse. Ours is simple, One Dog, one message, pees ever after. Our holy book is straightforward and simple to understand. It was written by one dog, St. Bernard, so there is no literary bickering to confuse us. *(I have Sandy to thank for the St. Bernard reference. Royalties on the way.)* Yes, we have pees ever after – EXCEPT when Liverpool lose and Shankly goes off on one – there's no peace at all then. Nothing can stop him. He's like a one-dog crusade. The only safe way to calm him down is to remind him of verse six, chapter three in our bible – 'Dogma for Beginners.' I quote: 'And Dog Almighty said, live and let Liverpool.'

Holiday Time

I was walking with Monica (Husky) and we were chatting about seasonal holidays. Such as Christmas, when the world goes potty for a couple of months. The focus of all the Upright's attention is on a fat red bloke who flies through the air in a wheelbarrow, pulled by a deer called Rude Olf. I asked Monica what it was like in her house. 'Mad,' she said, 'and annoying. I know I'm going to have to mentally hunker down when they put my bed in the hallway to make room for a flashing tree. Why the hell don't they put the tree in the hall so I can carry on watching TV?'

Monica was on the end of a long lead, about ten metres in front of her Upright, so she and I could talk freely without causing offense. Dad rarely has me on a lead, quite happy to let me socialize and wander off to mix with who I want, except when Dolly and Dibble are out. They are Dobermans, big things, bred for attack, not sitting in your lap. To make matters worse, Dolly has a psychological irregularity. Sometimes they're both off lead and they are never muzzled. The last thing you want is ten stone of psychopathic Dolly running loose. Particularly when McTavish starts yelling insults in the Gaelic tongue.

Monica is on a lead because of her breed's tendency to start running and only stop when it's tea time, which could mean twenty miles away! They also have a highly developed 'prey-drive,' which isn't ideal in a field full of family pets. I'm sure she wouldn't hurt anyone but she is tarred with the brush of her breed. Bert walked past, on the lookout for a turd. He was followed and watched closely by his Upright who would rather prevent an indiscretion than give Bert another tooth-brushing on their return home.

'I can't believe how much they spend on food, most of which is crammed into the fridge and freezer,' continued Monica. 'The daft thing is that everybody ends up starving because Ma Upright won't let anybody eat anything. "Don't touch that," she yelled, "that's for Christmas." It's lucky my Dad stashed some chocolate digestives in his shed or the poor lad could have starved to death. There's only four of them in the household, plus me. One of them is four years old and another ninety-three so they're hardly likely to make much of a dent on the food mountain, are they? All they need now is a power cut to really put the tin lid on it! We'd have molten e-numbers all over the ground floor. The plus side of their stupidity is that there's always the chance of left-overs.'

I have to agree with her - there's excess in the normal course of events, but holiday time it goes potty. They have similar in the States. Dad has recently reconnected with an old school friend who's now living stateside (hear that? hip talk, too!). I think he lives in that bit down the bottom that looks like a schlong (aka clock with a letter missing). Anyway, they have this thing that used to be called Thanksgiving. It's now called Thanksreceiving because it's more in line with what people seem to care about these days. Gimee, gimee, gimme. All mine, all mine. Ta very much. See ya. I 'thought' this about America, I didn't say it. Not sure why. Perhaps I've been drawn in to the 'mustn't offend at any cost' mentality. I didn't used to be like that; I used to call a spade a shovel and point out that my shovel could dig a hole to bury you in if you disagreed with me. Metaphorically, of course – usually.

Monica hasn't been here that long and in a non-sequitur, quite out of the blue, she said, 'You know, Frank, I enjoy living here. I feel good. Not because I fit in or anything, just that so far no-one has called me a twat.' I was rather surprised by her sudden change of direction, and her language, but replied, 'Well, that's nice Monica. There are few things better than people not calling you a twat.'
   Sorry for the ripe language, but it's what she said and I thought it worth repeating. It's all part of our rich and varied culture. Another brick in the pantheon that is our ethnology. Blimey, that's quite a sentence isn't it – verging on the literary!

Naughty words used in humour or for emphasis are acceptable, I think. Of course, if you're offended, please don't read the previous couple of paragraphs. Actually, I have had to exercise caution while repeating Shankly's exchanges; some of the language therein is too fruity for even the most liberal-minded. Football speak with a scouse inflection is as fruity as it gets.

Lucy joined us for a furlong or two. She was sober as a judge because the pubs had yet to open. She recalled an early Christmas. 'I remember being happy for Ronald, my little Upright, when he was only about six. He got new a bike and he was so excited. I'll never forget the innocent fun as he rode it around the neighbourhood. I used to run alongside him. I'd get a squeaky toy and be just as happy throwing that in the air and catching it, or have Ronald throw it round the lawn for me to chase.' She paused. 'We used to play hopscotch, too. It was a bit of a struggle for me with four legs, but it made him happy. A bit different this Christmas - Ronald's got a gaming box of some sort. I can hardly chase that, can I? No squeaky toy for me either. Though Betty bought me a corkscrew. Not sure whether that was generous or ironic.' As the clock struck twelve, Lucy broke off at a tangent and set off towards the Red Lion and an opportunity to cope with her memories.

I continued round with Monica when she suddenly burst into laughter. It coincided with us passing Doug the Pug. Because it's Christmas time, his Upright had dressed him in a red coat and plonked some sort of fatuous hat on his head with flashing red lights. Monica's laugh was a bit infectious and I joined in. 'Nice one, Doug,' I shouted to our friend. 'Very festive!'

'Bugger off,' he muttered.

We were chuckling as Monica said to me, 'Imagine a few thousand years ago when we were basically a single breed - a wolf-like creature that roamed wild and free. Then one winter, just after Uprights first appeared, something happened to change the course of our evolution. A pair of wolves saw the Uprights had fire. Not only were they keeping warm, they were also cooking roast lamb. Wolf number one said, "Come on, let's go and say hello, see if we can go and get warm and share their feast. What have we got to lose?" So, in they go and engage in the first contact between wolf and Upright. Fast-forward ten thousand years.' She laughed again, then pointed to Doug in his red coat and flashing hat. 'THAT is what we had to lose!'

Doug turned and scowled, not realizing he had been instrumental in changing the course of canine history. We'd had an OK couple of hours but now it had started raining. Believe it or not, the weather was worse than usual, the rain and wind seemed incessant. Sam was trying to keep us cheerful by singing, 'I'm dreaming of a wet Christmas.'

Doug was having none of it and shuffled off, head down. Don't know if he realized, but his head lights had gone out. Water in the workings, I suspect.

McTavish Wisdom

2022 is coming to an end and the Uprights are approaching another excuse to get pickled. They seem to fall into two factions come the year end - those who go out and enjoy themselves and Mum and Dad. No, that's not really fair; they've done their share of socialising over the years. Now, in the autumn of their years, it's time to save up for their retirement where they'll do even less than they do at present. I think I've mentioned this before somewhere, but Dad has been known to return home after a session on the wine with a U.D.I. aka, an Unidentified Drinking Injury. He has this self-defeating philosophy: Drinking red wine gives you the invincibility from the effects of drinking too much red wine. Which is all well and good except for the bruises or scrapes of unknown origin obtained back in the Mists of Merlot. Mmm. Mists of Merlot. Nice phrase, isn't it?

   He came staggering in the other night after a losing game of snooker with his brother - yet again. Mum asked him if he'd had a good game. He obviously wanted to forget about his sporting shortcomings so changed the subject. He said at random, 'Do you know we have a private investigator locally who lives in a tree? He's called Hercule Parrot.' Even Mum had to smile at that. Not only does excess wine cause injury, it also appears to unleash previously hidden creativity. At least that's what Dad tells us. He keeps giving it a try anyway!

Fireworks are a New Year celebration that some of us canines could do without. They don't bother me but some of my mates have a pathological hatred of them. I know some even have to have tranquilizers. Dad usually slips a slug of Crème de menthe into my water, which seems to do the trick. It tastes vile but I don't half see see some fancy flashing lights.

New Year. A time, according to Mum, for new resolutions. Lose a little weight perhaps, get a little fitter, learn a language. According to Dad, it's the chance to buy a decent bottle of wine and watch Jools Holland. 'Think longer term,' says Mum, 'set yourself a target of some kind.'

'I could try and cycle across the country,' he said.

'Go on then, off you go.' she says, suddenly excited.

'I can't. It'll take lots of planning.'

'Oh, pleeeease.'

'You can't just set off on a jaunt like that. However much you want me out of your way. Accommodation, battery charging, route, food, drink, all needs careful consideration.'

'You'd better get help then.'

So another year draws to a close where he's under her feet.

Another area where dogs are superior to Uprights is image. Basically, we just be ourselves, while they seem to have a need to fit in. McTavish, in philosopher mode, came up with an interesting comment the other day which got the jungle drums beating round the fields. He said: 'It's more difficult to be yourself than to conform.'

The more I thought about this the more I think he's right. I re-posted it in a bush a couple of days ago and the consensus is that a) there's no way that's an original McTavish, and b) whoever said it is probably correct. I'm not sure it's an original quote or whether he pinched it from The Wag, but it's a good one.

I think canines, because we're bred to do specific tasks, find it easier to be ourselves. We seem to be largely content with our lot. Of course, there's the odd awkward one who refuses to accept their position in life. I'm thinking of Shankly here, who reinvented himself as a noisy but basically clueless football pundit when he could have had a comfortable, cosseted existence as a lap dog.

The difference is that Uprights come into the world with a blank slate and have to find a direction. Most of them don't manage it because they end up being pushed or cajoled towards a target that often doesn't suit them. That's professionally, religiously and these days what pronoun they want to be referred to by. They have created difficulties for themselves by inventing wilder and wilder philosophies that they label under freedom. In fact, freedom is the last thing most of them find because they are restrained by a set of asphyxiating conventions. They come into the world screaming and defecating and it doesn't seem to get a lot better.

Dad started off on the wrong foot in a bakery, tried again, then again and finally semi-retired with a catalogue of cock-ups in his rear-view mirror. Now he writes books that nobody reads and builds fences for old ladies. Literally, not metaphorically.

One of the tricks to happiness is being happy with what we have because by constantly striving for something better, we'll never be content. There's always something bigger, and usually that something is much more expensive. Maybe you want it because your neighbour has it, or someone on TV, but the way to madness is knowing that the one thing you REALLY want is always just out of reach. It's easy to compromise today for something that's out of reach. I'm not saying don't have ambition, but the trick is to recognize the point where you're content. Hamilton, in his no-nonsense way, says that trying to make sense of our confusing world is like trying to shoot a cloud from the sky. Best to not even try.

Recreation is one thing the Uprights undertake. Oh dear, undertake - rather an unfortunate choice of word there. Looking at some of the the puce complexions we see as they struggle up local hills, an undertaker may be on duty sooner rather than later. One sport they seem to enjoy is bowling, an activity they can do well into their senior years. We smile as we pass the bowling green and hear the creaks and groans of senior players bending down to retrieve their woods. Oofs and aaahs are the soundtrack of elderly Uprights keeping themselves in prime condition. As prime as age allows. Mind you, Dad makes plenty senior noises just walking!

Canines are basically easy-going, restrained creatures, but there is one area that can cause conflict. That's when a new mini-Upright comes into a household. Suddenly all the attention is on the mini and the dog can feel left out in the cold. We get on well with minis on the whole and are often protective of them but we can end up seriously short of attention. We try all sorts to get the Upright's attention. Lying on our backs waggling our legs about, barking at shadows, jumping on and off the furniture. It's a bit of a balancing act because if we overdo it we can get booted out into the garden. The trick seems to be to target the male

Uprights, because they have less of a hands-on role, particularly when the infant is squawking or shitting everywhere. The male suddenly finds he needs to go and change the oil in the car and we can go and keep him company. If there is a consolation, it's that while attention is on the mini we can raid the larder.

Bruce and Shanks

Dad bought an electric bike while the world was in lockdown. A move that appeared to be straight out of the Upright's 'Doesn't Appear to Make Much Sense' manual; in other words, spending a small fortune on something when he can't even go out on it. Eventually of course we were all released and the world creaked back into life again. Dad had spent the time he was locked up by practicing getting in and out his cycle shorts - which proved more difficult than it sounds. He always did it in the privacy of his room and we could hear regular bangs and thumps as he fell over one way or another trying to get his legs in. In fact, he got so much exercise squeezing himself into his Lycra that he needn't have bought the bike at all. But he had, so then he had to buy all sorts of extras. Necessary investments, he says, tools of the trade required by the elite athlete. 'In that case,' Mum said, with a certain logic, 'you can save yourself some money?' Which was a bit unkind. If true.

She has a point of course, but I admire Dad having a go. He bought a drinks bottle for his wine, a rear light in case he ends up going backwards when going uphill and an extremely unpleasant day-glo jacket, in lime green. He looks like an avocado atop a tangly assortment of random metal bits, and there's a worrying little squeak coming from somewhere near his right knee.

I take the mickey out of him but I know he's a bit shaky physically and has to keep moving. Like some sharks, that need to constantly move to keep oxygenated water flowing though their gills. Dad's like that, if you replace the water with Merlot. He has to keep moving down to the off-license. Oxygenated Merlot is 'part of the elite athlete's dietary regimen,' he says. Truth be known, he's not exactly shark-like; he's rather slower and less threatening. In fact, less well evolved altogether. He works within restrictive parameters, but does manage to make a little progress. Occasionally.

Here is what he said not long ago: *'Though every step is inevitably a step nearer my demise, it's also paradoxically a step towards avoiding it. When diagnosed with knackered arteries, I was frightened. I could imagine the grim reaper, in the gloom of the predawn, peering down from the hill to my left as I pass the wood where the rabbits have been annihilated by the foxes. Today I march past with determined gait to deny the reaper another soul. Twin battles - the reaper and me for my soul, the dog and me for my sanity.'* Quite deep, really. It's meant he's re-focused his outlook. He thinks that by walking in the dark the reaper won't spot him. 'Planning for my retirement is a simple thing,' he says. 'I simply plan to get a day older each day.'

He's quite conscious of his diet and, as he points out, twenty years ago TVs were fat and people thin. Now it's the other way round. And it's ironic that crisps (or chips as they are called Stateside), a snack you eat while slobbing around in a chair watching daytime TV, are called 'Walkers'. If they'd have called them 'Trotters' perhaps the Uprights would have been collectively fitter.

Speaking of that, Bruce the Lurcher has been entered into a race. The Littleborough and District 500-yard dash is a sprint down the canal for, well, anyone who can sprint. So it's not for me. If there was a 500-yard amble, I'd be there in a flash. Unfortunately these days I run like the winded. The prize is a years' supply of chicken sponsored by a local butcher so it's worth Bruce putting in the hard yards and doing some training. I really want him to win of course, but I would be slightly envious, for a year at least, while he dines on chicken as I plough through my horse. Can you plough through a horse?

Bruce asked McTavish what he was doing today. 'Nothing,' replies McTavish, 'it's my day off.'
  'I need someone to work the stopwatch and time some runs.'
  'When you ask me what I am doing today, and I say "nothing," it does not mean I am free. It means I am doing nothing.'
  'But the race is next Tuesday and I need to know where I'm at.'
  'At? I'll tell you where you're at. You're at the point of cheesing me right off.'
  'It's because you can't run faster than a three-legged sloth, isn't it?'
  'Get Shankly to do it, he's sporty.' Which is why we find Shankly is sitting on top of a pair of step ladders yelling instructions at Bruce.

I'm watching from the sidelines with Bert. Both of us have sympathy with poor old Bruce. 'He'll have to go that extra mile in training if he's going to win,' said Bert.

Sam sidled up and said, 'The only time Bruce went the extra mile was when he missed his motorway exit. He's no chance; there are greyhounds and whippets racing in peak condition.'

Nevertheless, Bruce did enter and, against the odds, Bruce did win. Mysteriously, the two favourites, Greyhound Roger and Willy the Whippet, both failed to make the start line. Both came down with a tummy upset and when the starting pistol fired they were indisposed down the canal bank.

On the start line, a second or two before the race, Bruce looked over to his trainer. Shankly had agreed to become Bruce's official mentor in exchange for 50% of any prize money. Shankly gave Bruce a big scouse wink as the gun fired. Bruce leapt off the line and romped to victory.

'Nobbled we were,' said Willy, as he walked home unsteadily. 'That bloody Scouser slipped something in the water in the weighing room.'

Under the heading, *'The 2022 500-yard dash'*, Bruce's name entered the history books as winner and another chapter of scheming and conniving came to a close.

Year End

I remember Mum telling me the story of when she was cutting my predecessor's hair. This was before my time, when they were traveling down from Holland to France. She was a Collie/Retriever cross, although, because she lived in France, she called herself a Bordeaux Collie. She was called Bonny and had thick hair so tackling it was rather an ordeal for both mother and dog. They were in port in a place called Saint Quentin, northern France, and Mum was cutting Bonny on the flat bed of a trailer parked nearby. It was a good height for Mum, who has a dodgy back. Amazingly, flying overhead was the Patrouille Acrobatique, the French equivalent of our Red Arrows. They were doing some training and Mum and Bonny were their only audience. Quite a privilege that must have been.

BUT - the planes must have distracted Mum because the guard came off the clippers without her noticing. As a result, Bonny ended up with a big stripe down her flank where the fur was hacked off to the skin. I suppose it could have been trendy in fashionable Paris, where anything goes, but here in a little port in the middle of France, it looked a bit daft. I've seen the photo. I've been taken to a professional groomers to have mine done. Another expense Dad grumbles about. But they do a decent job, even if the lass does have to put a muzzle on me when she cuts my feet. I'm a bit sensitive down there.

Dad cuts his own hair with clippers and a number one guard. It looks awful, frankly, and more than once Mum has threatened to call out the Hair Ambulance. He certainly isn't one of those who keeps up with trends and fashions. In fact he calls himself a sartorial datum point – an untidy heap against which all other incarnations of appearance may be judged. At least he can laugh about it.

Most of us come out New Year's Eve. There are piddles galore as each of us wish the others luck for the forthcoming endurance test that will be another year. I know Dad and me will have battles, but if we can stay focused we'll get by and still be friends. It's up to him to back down. I won't!

One thing I'll definitely have to address next year, and SOON, is his technique for drying me off after a damp walk. He uses a towel (often warmed on the radiator) and is actually pretty thorough, but – BIG BUT – when he dries my hind legs, he gets rather too close to my 'south pole' for comfort. I get nervous ... think dogtor ... think Boggart! Anyhow, I mustn't let my thoughts spoil our last potter of the year.

Late in the day, Lucy is a bit wobbly due to a session in the Red Lion. Bruce looks like he's developed lumbago after his racing exploits. Shankly is like the dog that got the cream because he's got six months of succulent chicken to look forward to. To get away from fresh meat envy, Sam tells us he's off to watch a vegetarian tribute band called Quorn. Do we believe him? I don't think so. Betty the Dalmatian and Alice Aforethought are elegance personified as they glide over the turf, promenading. They are chatting in hushed tones, probably plotting how to relieve Shankly of some chicken. Julie went into labour a couple of hours ago so there will be the pitter patter of puppy's dog turds come the new year. Monica went with her to offer moral support. Doug the Pug and McTavish are chuckling about Doug getting the last laugh with his non-flashing Christmas hat. He flogged it to a Pomeranian called Edward who'd wandered into the shire and got fleeced. Oh hello, there's my mate Lad. He's a large sheep dog who has had a bad back recently and been hors de combat. Good to see him about again. He's been well cared for, his Mum and Dad even took him to a dog swimming pool called *'Doggy Paddle'*. It was water therapy to get him fit again. There's dear old Bert is on the prowl for a final snack of 2022 and Mad Lynn the Afghan is brushing her hair in a rose bush outside number 22. Thank goodness Dolly and Dibble are under lock and key.

This time of year we remember our friends who have crossed the bridge. There's Bonny and Treasure, Solo, Barney and Vinny. Their scents are no more but their spirits fly free over our park and playing fields. We can sense them and see them run, forever young, free of worldly constraint. We know they are there and we know they are happy.

Gradually the field empties as we all go and wait for an Upright called Big Ben to usher in a new year. As I go through the gate, I turn and see the solitary figure of Alfred the King Charles up by the goal posts. I've no idea what he's doing. I saw him watching Bruce's race from a canal bridge so I suspect he's praying to Dog

Almighty, asking if he can have a bit more speed. Dear old Alfred. In a world of his own at times. Or perhaps he's in someone else's world – rather like the rest of us.

The End

About the Author

This refers to Jo May, not Frank!

I live in Littleborough with my wife Janna and dog whose real name is Tache. I changed the name to Frank because calling a book *Let's be Tache* wouldn't make much sense.

Jan and I have both lived here on and off for over 60 years.

I began writing monthly articles for a canal magazine in 2007. Catastrophically (for the magazine), following an editorial misunderstanding, we parted company. Yes, I was sacked. I began to chronicle our travels which ultimately resulted in my three 'At Large' books, beginning with *'A Narrowboat at Large.'* I describe the books as a huge collection of warm memories, a library on which Jan and I can draw during long winter evenings and which will help us through our rocking-chair years. Magical times.

After destroying the UK's canal infrastructure on two narrowboats and rearranging a fair amount of continental waterways heritage on a rusty old Dutch Barge, our boating days came to an end in 2015, to everyone's relief except ours.

Boating days behind me, my new challenge is an e-bike. However, to mix metaphors, it's not all been plain sailing. *A Bike at Large* is written in homage to all portly, sub-standard cyclists, of which I am one. *Ordeals on Wheels* sums it up quite nicely.

I've also written three novels in addition to my two little books, namely The Boro and this little book of doggy memories.

You can connect with me on:

🌐 https://jomay.uk

📘 https://www.facebook.com/jotheboat

Also by Jo May

Let's be Frank is my second mini book.
 It is written through the eyes of my dog.
 (Though Frank insists he wrote it himself).
 It's a dog's eye view of our crazy world.

My first mini book is called *The Boro, Now and Then*. See below.
 A third 'mini' is in the writing. Working title, *'Dogs, Gods and Odds and sods'*

My 'At Large' series comprises three boating books and a cycling one:
 A Narrowboat at Large (below)
 A Barge at Large
 A Barge at Large II
 A Bike at Large

Three novels:
 Operation Vegetable
 Twice Removed
 Flawed Liaisons

They are all here on my website: jomay.uk

The Boro. Now and Then

Returning to Littleborough after a break of nearly thirty years, I hope nothing's changed. But, inevitably, it has.

Like many folk in their seventh decade, I'm haunted by the spectre of how good things used to be.

It takes me a while, but I realize the past mustn't dominate; it must don a pair of slippers, settle into a comfy armchair and watch our future unfold. We have to create a new now in a place we're happy to live, both geographically and emotionally.

These impressions of a chap battling to blend with a modern world are also my light-hearted and daft take on a place I love, and dedicated to the memories of times gone by and for tomorrow.

Printed in Great Britain
by Amazon